G.W. Bartle

# An Epitome of English Grammar

SALZWASSER
VERLAG

G.W. Bartle

# An Epitome of English Grammar

Reprint of the original, first published in 1859.

1st Edition 2022  |  ISBN: 978-3-37513-154-8

Verlag (Publisher): Salzwasser Verlag GmbH, Zeilweg 44, 60439 Frankfurt, Deutschland
Vertretungsberechtigt (Authorized to represent): E. Roepke, Zeilweg 44, 60439 Frankfurt, Deutschland
Druck (Print): Books on Demand GmbH, In de Tarpen 42, 22848 Norderstedt, Deutschland

# AN
# EPITOME
## OF
# ENGLISH GRAMMAR.

### INTENDED FOR

### SCHOOLS AND PRIVATE FAMILIES.

BY

## G. W. BARTLE, T.C.D.

Author of an "ELEMENTARY TREATISE ON ARITHMETIC,"

ETC., ETC.

LONDON:
PIPER, STEPHENSON, AND SPENCE.

LIVERPOOL:
EDWARD HOWELL, 6, CHURCH-STREET.

1858.

# PREFACE.

———o———

THE following questions and answers on ENGLISH GRAMMAR have been drawn up by the Author with the sole intention of presenting to the juvenile mind, in as few words as possible, the substance of the Etymology and Syntax of his native Language, so that the pupil may not be obliged to cram his memory, and tax it with a mass of unnecessary matter. The experienced Teacher knows well that every branch of Education, depending chiefly upon the memory, cannot be more easily and effectually learnt than by question and answer; nor is this plan found useful to School Boys only, but it is also highly serviceable to those who are considerably advanced in their academic studies. The Author is of opinion, that if any one will take a little trouble to make himself thoroughly master of what is here submitted to his notice, he will be fully prepared to peruse any Grammar of the Language, and at the same time to understand it.

Throughout the present epitome the Author has always endeavored to hold the substance and reject the shadow ; to keep the corn, and burn the chaff; and he hopes that a perusal of the Book will clearly show that Truth authorised him to make such a statement.

# AN EPITOME

OF

# ENGLISH GRAMMAR.

———o———

Q. What is the use of English Grammar?

A. It shows how to speak and write the English language properly.

Q. Into what number of parts is it divided?

A. Four; namely, Orthography, Etymology, Prosody, and Syntax.

Q. How many letters are there in the English alphabet?

A. Twenty-six.

Q. Can you tell me the derivation of the word alphabet?

B

A. It is derived from the first two letters of the Greek alphabet, namely, *alpha* and *beta*.

Q. Are the twenty-six letters divided into classes?

A. Yes; into vowels and consonants.

Q. Which are the vowels?

A. *A, e, i, o, u,* and *w* and *y* when they terminate a word or syllable.

Q. What are the rest of the letters called?

A. Consonants; because they are sounded together with vowels.

Q. What is a dipththong?

A. Two vowels united, as *oa* in the word moan.

Q. What is a triphthong?

A. Three vowels united, as *eau* in beauty.

Q. What is a monosyllable?

A. A word of one syllable.

Q. What is a dissyllable?

A. A word of two syllables.

Q. What is a polysyllable?

A. A word of four or more syllables.

Q. Explain what is meant by Etymology?

A. It is that division of the Grammar which shows the difference in the parts of speech and the changes they undergo.

Q. How many different sorts of words does the English language contain?

A. Nine; known by the names of Article, Noun or Substantive, Adjective, Pronoun, Verb, Adverb, Preposition, Conjunction, and Interjection.

## ARTICLE.

Q. What is an article?

A. An article is a word placed before nouns, and it limits the extension of the nouns; as, *a* man.

Q. How many articles are there in English?

A. Two; *a* and *the*.

Q. When do we use *an* instead of *a*?

A. When the noun before which it is placed begins with a vowel or silent *h*.

Q. Will you please to give me an example?

A. Instead of saying *a* apple, we say *an* apple, because the noun apple begins with a vowel; but we say *a* book and not *an* book, because book begins with a consonant; and also, instead of saying *a* honest man, we say *an* honest man, because the *h* in honest is silent.

Q. Why is *a* called the indefinite article?

A. Because it never points out any one thing distinctly from another thing.

Q. Does *the* point out one thing distinctly?

A. Yes; and on this account it is called the definite article.

## NOUN or SUBSTANTIVE.

Q. What is a noun?

A. Anything that can be conceived to have an independent existence; as, man, virtue.

Q. How many kinds of nouns are there?

A. Six; namely, proper, common, abstract, collective, verbal, and compound.

Q. Please to show me the difference of these nouns?

A. *London* is a *proper* noun, because it belongs especially to the capital of England.

*City* is a *common* noun, because it can be applied to any city, as the *city* of London, *city* of Paris. *Virtue* is an *abstract* noun, because, considered abstractly. *An army* is a *collective* noun, because a number of individuals are spoken of as if only one. *Reading* is a *verbal* noun, because derived from the verb *to read*. *Drawing-room* is a *compound* noun, because it consists of two words, namely, *drawing* and *room*.

## NUMBER.

Q. What do you mean by number?

A. I mean the difference between one and more than one.

Q. What is one called?

A. One is called *singular*; and any number above one is called *plural*.

Q. Why?

A. Because it is more than one.

Q. How many numbers have nouns?

A. Two; namely, *singular* and *plural*.

Q. How do you convert a noun singular into a noun plural?

A. Mostly by adding *s* to the singular : as, *book* is singular ; but if I put *s* to it, it becomes plural.

Q. Are all nouns pluralized in the same way ?

A. No ; those nouns ending in *s*, *ss*, *ch*, *x*, *sh*, or *o* are made plural by adding *es*, instead of *s* ; as, *church, churches ; miss, misses.*

Q. Suppose those nouns ending in *ch* have the *ch* sounded like *k*, how then do you make the singular plural ?

A. By adding *s* only ; as, *monarch, monarchs.*

Q. How are the nouns pluralized if they end in *f* or *fe?*

A. By changing *f* or *fe* into *ves ;* as, *life, lives ; loaf, loaves.*

Q. How do you pluralize those ending in *y ?*

A. By changing *y* into *ies*, if the *y* be preceded by a consonant, and by adding *s* only if the *y* follow a vowel : as, *lady, ladies ; day, days.*

Q. Let me hear you make the following nouns, plural : Pen, ink, boot, church, stomach, fox, baby, loaf, sugar, life, wish ?

## GENDER.

Q. What is to be understood by *gender?*

A. It shows the difference in the sexes.

Q. How many genders are there?

A. Three; namely, *masculine, feminine,* and *neuter.*

Q. To what is the word *masculine* applied?

A. It is applied to all *male* animals; as, *man, bull.* *Feminine* is applied to *female* animals; as, *woman, hen, cow.* *Neuter* is applied to things void of life; as, *wood, ink.*

Q. Tell me the gender of the following nouns: Man, woman, book, cow, bull, hen, ink, milk.

## CASE.

Q. How many *cases* have nouns?

A. Three; namely, *nominative, possessive,* and *objective.*

Q. What is the difference of these cases?

A. The *nominative* and *objective* are alike in appearance, but occupy different places in a sentence; while the *possessive* is formed from the nominative by adding *s* and a little mark ('), called apostrophe.

Q. How do you go through a noun in this way?

A. We say—

|  | Singular. | Plural. |
|---|---|---|
| *Nominative.* | Boy. | Boys. |
| *Possessive.* | Boy's. | Boys'. |
| *Objective.* | Boy. | Boys. |

Q. Decline the following: Book, girl, father, mother, sister.

## ADJECTIVE.

Q. What is an adjective?

A. A word put to a noun to tell us what sort of a noun it is; as, a *good* man.

Q. Which is the adjective in the example just given?

A. Good.

Q. Why?

A. Because it tells me what sort of a man he is; namely, a *good* man, and not a *bad* one.

Q. How many degrees of comparison have adjectives?

A. Three; namely, *positive, comparative,* and *superlative.*

Q. What is the difference of these three words?

A. The *positive* simply expresses the quality, as, a *good* man; the *comparative* adds or takes away a degree, as, a *better* man; while the *superlative* raises the noun to the highest point, or sinks it to the lowest, as, the *best* man, or the *worst* man.

Q. How do you compare adjectives?

A. If they consist of one syllable, they are compared by adding *r* or *er* to the positive degree; *st* or *est* to the superlative: as, *fine, finer, finest.* If the adjective be a word of more than one syllable, it must be compared by adding *more* and *most*; as, virtuous, *more* virtuous, *most* virtuous.

## PRONOUNS.

Q. What is a pronoun?

A. It is a word put in the place of a noun, in

order that the noun may not be repeated too often; as, John is good, because *he* obeys his parents.

Q. How are pronouns divided?

A. Into three kinds; namely, *personal, relative*, and *adjective*.

Q. How many *personal* pronouns are there?

A. Five; namely, *I, thou, he, she*, and *it*.

Q. Which are the pronouns of the first person?

A. *I* and *we.*

Q. Which are those of the second person?

A. *Thou*, and *ye* or *you.*

Q. Which are the third personal pronouns?

A. *He, she, it*, and *they.*

Q. How do you decline the *personal* pronouns?

A. In the following manner:

|  | *Singular.* | *Plural.* |
|---|---|---|
| *Nominative.* | I. | We. |
| *Possessive.* | Mine. | Ours. |
| *Objective.* | Me. | Us. |
| *Nominative.* | Thou. | Ye or you. |
| *Possessive.* | Thine. | Yours. |
| *Objective.* | Thee. | You. |

|  | *Singular.* | *Plural.* |
|---|---|---|
| *Nominative.* | He. | They. |
| *Possessive.* | His. | Theirs. |
| *Objective.* | Him. | Them. |
| *Nominative.* | She. | They. |
| *Possessive.* | Hers. | Theirs. |
| *Objective.* | Her. | Them. |

Q. How do you decline the pronoun *It?*

| *Nominative.* | It. | They. |
|---|---|---|
| *Possessive.* | Its. | Theirs. |
| *Objective.* | It. | Them. |

Q. What person is *I?*

A. The first.

Q. What person is *Thou?*

A. The second; and the other three are all of the third person, because spoken of.

Q. What do you mean by *relative* pronouns?

A. They are words relating to other words which precede them, and which are called the *antecedents.*

Q. What is the meaning of antecedent?

A. It signifies going before.

Q. Please tell me the simple relative pronouns?

A. They are, *who, which,* and *that.*

Q. Are there any more?

A. Yes: one which is a *compound* relative; namely, the word *what.*

Q. Why is it called compound?

A. Because it includes two words, the antecedent and the relative pronoun.

Q. How do you decline the relative pronoun *who?*

A. In the following manner:

|  | *Singular.* |
| --- | --- |
| *Nominative.* | Who. |
| *Possessive.* | Whose. |
| *Objective.* | Whom. |

Q. How many kinds of *adjective* pronouns are there?

A. Four; namely, *possessive, demonstrative, distributive,* and *indefinite.*

Q. Will you mention the *possessive?*

A. They are, *my, thy, his, her, our, your, their, its, own.*

Q. I wish to know the *distributive* pronouns?

A. *Each, every, either*, and *neither*.

Q. Which are the *demonstrative?*

A. *This* and *that*, with their plurals, *these* and *those*.

Q. Which are the *indefinite* pronouns?

A. They are *none, any, some, both, all, such, one, another, other, whole*.

Q. Are there any other kinds of pronouns not hitherto mentioned?

A. Yes; some *compound* pronouns; as, *myself, thyself, himself*, and *themselves*.

## THE VERB.

Q. What is a verb?

A. A verb is the principal word in every sentence, and denotes either existence, action, or passion; and always signifies being, doing, or suffering something.

Q. How many sorts of verbs are there?

A. Three; namely, *active, passive*, and *neuter*.

Q. Explain what you mean by an *active* verb?

A. By an *active* verb, I mean one which passes from an agent to an object ; as, John *broke* the window.

Q. Which is the verb in the sentence just given ?

A. *Broke* ; and is active, because it passes from the agent John to the window, and breaks it.

Q, What do you mean by a *neuter* verb ?

A. By a *neuter* verb, I mean one which does not leave the agent to pass to an object ; as, James *sleeps.* Here, it is obvious, that the sleeping is confined to James, and does not pass to any other person or thing.

Q. What is to be understood by a *passive* verb?

A. A *passive* verb denotes enduring of what is done to you by another ; as, I am *wounded* by John.

Q. Which are the *auxiliary* verbs ?

A. *Shall will, may, can, must, have, do, might, would, could,* and *should.*

Q. How are verbs inflected ?

A. By *moods, tenses, numbers, persons,* and *voices.*

Q. What is the meaning of *tense?*

A. Tense means time.

Q. What does *present* tense mean?

A. Present tense means present time.

Q. How do you conjugate a regular verb?

A. I conjugate a regular verb in the following manner.

Q. But before you show me how you conjugate a regular verb, will you please to inform me what you mean by *conjugating* a verb?

A. By *conjugating* a verb, I mean putting the verb through its different moods, tenses, persons, and numbers.

Let us go through the *regular* verb
*to advise.*

### INDICATIVE MOOD.

Q. What is the *present tense* of the verb *to advise?*

| Singular. | Plural. |
|---|---|
| A. I advise. | We advise. |
| Thou advisest. | You or ye advise. |
| He advises. | They advise. |

Q. What is the *past tense* of the same verb?

| Singular. | Plural. |
|---|---|
| A. I advised. | We advised. |
| Thou advisedst. | You advised. |
| He advised. | They advised. |

Q. What is the *perfect tense?*

| Singular. | Plural. |
|---|---|
| A. I have advised. | We have advised. |
| Thou hast advised. | You have advised. |
| He has advised. | They have advised. |

Q. What is the *pluperfect tense?*

| Singular. | Plural. |
|---|---|
| A. I had advised. | We had advised. |
| Thou hadst advised. | You had advised. |
| He had advised. | They had advised. |

Q. What is the *first future tense?*

A.—

| Singular. | Plural. |
|---|---|
| I shall or will advise. | We shall or will advise. |
| Thou shalt or wilt advise. | You shall or will advise. |
| He shall or will advise. | They shall or will advise. |

Q. What is the second *future tense?*

A.—

| Singular. | Plural. |
|---|---|
| I shall have advised. | We shall or will have advised. |
| Thou shalt or wilt have advised. | You shall or will have advised. |
| He shall or will have advised. | They shall or will have advised. |

## POTENTIAL MOOD.

Q. What is the *present tense* of this mood?

A.—

| Singular. | Plural. |
|---|---|
| I may, can, or must advise. | We may, can, or must advise. |
| Thou mayst, canst, or must advise. | You may, can, or must advise. |
| He may, can, or must advise. | They may, can, or must advise. |

Q. What is the *past tense ?*

A.—

| *Singular.* | *Plural.* |
|---|---|
| I might, could, would, or should advise. | We might, could, would, or should advise. |
| Thou mightest, could, would, or should advise. | You might, could, would, or should advise. |
| He might, could, would, or should advise. | They might, could, would, or should advise. |

Q. What is the *perfect tense ?*

A.—

| *Singular.* | *Plural.* |
|---|---|
| I may have advised. | We may have advised. |
| Thou mayest have advised. | You may have advised. |
| He may have advised. | They may have advised. |

Q. What is the *pluperfect tense ?*

A.—

| Singular. | Plural. |
|---|---|
| I might have advised. | We might have advised. |
| Thou mightst have advised. | You might have advised. |
| He might have advised. | They might have advised. |

## SUBJUNCTIVE MOOD.

Q. What is the *present tense* of this mood?

| Singular. | Plural. |
|---|---|
| A. If I advise. | If we advise. |
| If thou advise. | If you advise. |
| If he advise. | If they advise. |

## IMPERATIVE MOOD.

Q. What is the *present tense* of this mood?

A.—

| Singular. | Plural. |
|---|---|
| Let me advise. | Let us advise. |
| Advise thou, or do thou advise. | Advise you, or do you advise. |
| Let him advise. | Let them advise. |

C

### INFINITIVE MOOD.

Q. What is the *present* and *perfect tense* of this mood?

A. To advise.
To have advised.

Q. What are the *present, past,* and *perfect participles* of this verb?

A. Advising.
Advised.
Having advised.

Q. What benefit do you expect to derive from having learnt to conjugate this verb—to advise?

A. I expect that I can now conjugate any regular verb in the English language.

You are perfectly right: every regular verb is conjugated in the same way.

Q. What are the signs of all the *perfect tenses?*

A. Have.

Q. What are the signs of the *pluperpect?*

A. Had.

Q. What are the signs of the *first future?*

A. Shall and will.

Q. What are the signs of the *second future?*

A. Shall have and will have.

Q. What are the signs of the *present potential?*

A. May, can, and must.

Q. Name the signs of the *perfect potential?*

A. May have, must have, and can have.

Q. What are the signs of the *imperfect potential?*

A. Might, could, would, and should.

Q. What are the signs of the *pluperfect potential?*

A. Might have, could have, would have, and should have.

## THE VERB *to be.*

Q. Let me hear you conjugate the verb *to be?*

### INDICATIVE MOOD.

*Present Tense.*

| Singular. | Plural. |
|---|---|
| I am. | We are. |
| Thou art. | You are. |
| He is. | They are. |

### Past Tense.

| Singular. | Plural. |
|---|---|
| I was. | We were. |
| Thou wast. | You were. |
| He was. | They were. |

### Perfect Tense.

| Singular. | Plural. |
|---|---|
| I have been. | We have been. |
| Thou hast been. | You have been. |
| He has been. | They have been. |

### Pluperfect Tense.

| Singular. | Plural. |
|---|---|
| I had been. | We had been. |
| Thou hadst been. | You had been. |
| He had been. | They had been. |

### First Future Tense.

| Singular. | Plural. |
|---|---|
| I shall or will be. | We shall or will be. |
| Thou shalt or wilt be. | You shall or will be. |
| He shall or will be. | They shall or will be. |

## Second Future Tense.

| Singular. | Plural. |
|---|---|
| I shall or will have been. | We shall or will have been. |
| Thou shalt or wilt have been. | You shall or will have been. |
| He shall or will have been. | They shall or will have been. |

## POTENTIAL MOOD.

### Present Tense.

| Singular. | Plural. |
|---|---|
| I may be. | We may be. |
| Thou mayst be. | You may be. |
| He may be. | They may be. |

### Past Tense.

| Singular. | Plural. |
|---|---|
| I might be. | We might be. |
| Thou mightst be. | You might be. |
| He might be. | They might be. |

### Perfect Tense.

| Singular. | Plural. |
| --- | --- |
| I may have been. | We may been. |
| Thou mayst have been. | You may have been. |
| He may have been. | They may have been. |

### Pluperfect Tense.

| Singular. | Plural. |
| --- | --- |
| I might have been. | We might have been. |
| Thou mightst have been. | You might have been. |
| He might have been. | They might have been. |

## SUBJUNCTIVE MOOD.

### Present Tense.

| Singular. | Plural. |
| --- | --- |
| If I be. | If we be. |
| If thou be. | If you be. |
| If he be. | If they be. |

### Past Tense.

| Singular. | Plural. |
| --- | --- |
| If I were. | If we were. |
| If thou wert. | If you were. |
| If he were. | If they were. |

## IMPERATIVE MOOD.

| *Singular.* | *Plural.* |
|---|---|
| Let me be. | Let us be. |
| Be thou, or do thou be. | Be you, or do you be. |
| Let him be. | Let them be. |

## INFINITIVE MOOD.

*Present Tense.*

To be.

*Perfect Tense.*

To have been.

*Participles.*

| *Present.* | *Past.* | *Perfect.* |
|---|---|---|
| Being. | Been. | Having been. |

## PASSIVE VERB.

Q. How do you form a *passive* verb?

A. A *passive* verb is formed by placing the past participle of an *active* verb after the verb *to be;* as, *I am.* Now, take the past participle of the *active* verb *to advise*, and put it after *I am,* and it becomes *passive;* as, *I am advised.*

Q. Let me hear you go through a passive verb?

### Present Tense.

| Singular. | Plural. |
| --- | --- |
| I am advised. | We are advised. |
| Thou art advised. | You are advised. |
| He is advised. | They are advised. |

### Past Tense.

| Singular. | Plural. |
| --- | --- |
| I was advised. | We were advised. |
| Thou wast advised. | You were advised. |
| He was advised. | They were advised. |

### Perfect Tense.

| Singular. | Plural. |
| --- | --- |
| I have been advised. | We have been advised. |
| Thou hast been advised. | You have been advised. |
| He has been advised. | They have been advised. |

### Pluperfect Tense.

| Singular. | Plural. |
|---|---|
| I had been advised. | We had been advised. |
| Thou hadst been advised. | You had been advised. |
| He had been advised. | They had been advised. |

### First Future Tense.

| Singular. | Plural. |
|---|---|
| I shall or will be advised. | We shall or will be advised. |
| Thou shalt or wilt be advised. | You shall or will be advised. |
| He shall or will be advised. | They shall or will be advised. |

### Second Future Tense.

| Singular. | Plural. |
|---|---|
| I shall or will have been advised. | We shall or will have been advised. |
| Thou shalt or wilt have been advised. | You shall or will have been advised. |
| He shall or will have been advised. | They shall or will have been advised. |

## POTENTIAL MOOD.

### Present Tense.

| Singular. | Plural. |
|---|---|
| I may be advised. | We may be advised. |
| Thou mayst be advised. | You may be advised. |
| He may be advised. | They may be advised. |

### Past Tense.

| Singular. | Plural. |
|---|---|
| I might be advised. | We might be advised. |
| Thou mightst be advised. | You might be advised. |
| He might be advised. | They might be advised. |

### Perfect Tense.

| Singular. | Plural. |
|---|---|
| I may have been advised. | We may have been advised. |
| Thou mayst have been advised. | You may have been advised. |
| He may have been advised. | They may have been advised. |

### Pluperfect Tense.

*Singular.*

I might have been advised.

Thou mightst have been advised.

He might have been advised.

*Plural.*

We might have been advised.

You might have been advised.

They might have been advised.

### SUBJUNCTIVE MOOD.

#### Present Tense.

*Singular.*

If I be advised.

If thou be advised.

If he be advised.

*Plural.*

If we be advised.

If you be advised.

If they be advised.

#### Past Tense.

*Singular.*

If I were advised.

If thou wert advised.

If he were advised.

*Plural.*

If we were advised.

If you were advised.

If they were advised.

## IMPERATIVE MOOD.

| *Singular.* | *Plural.* |
|---|---|
| Let me be advised. | Let us be advised. |
| Be thou, or do thou be advised. | Be you, or do you be advised. |
| Let him be advised. | Let them be advised. |

## INFINITIVE MOOD.

### *Present Tense.*

To be advised.

### *Perfect Tense.*

To have been advised.

### *Participles.*

| *Present.* | *Past.* | *Perfect.* |
|---|---|---|
| Being advised. | Been advised. | Having been advised. |

Q. What is called the *emphatic* form of the verb?

A. When the principal verb is accompanied by the auxiliary verb *do;* as, *I do advise.*

Q. What is called the *progressive* form of the verb?

A. It is called a progressive form of the verb when the present participle follows the verb *To be;* as, *I am advising.*

## ADVERBS.

Q. What do you mean by an adverb?

A. By an adverb I mean a part of speech joined to a verb to qualify it in some way or other; as, James runs *well.*

Q. Which is the adverb in the sentence just laid down?

A. *Well* is the adverb, and it shows how James runs; namely, he runs *well.*

Q. To what parts of speech are adverbs in particular joined?

A. To three; namely, to adjectives, adverbs, and verbs.

Q. Give me an example of an adverb joined with an adjective?

A. *Very* beautiful; *very* being the adverb, and *beautiful* the adjective.

An example of one adverb with another; as, *Very well*, both being adverbs.

Q. Give me an example of an adverb joined with a verb?

A. He writes *badly; badly* is the adverb, joined with the verb *writes.*


## PREPOSITIONS.


Q. What is a preposition?

A. A Preposition is a part of speech put before *nouns*, to show some relation of place, and the like; as, *From* London; We went *from* London *to* Edinburgh.

Q. Which are the prepositions in the examples already given?

A. The prepositions are *to* and *from;* and the relationship between the two words is simply this, that *to* suggests *nearness* and *from* *distance.*

## CONJUNCTIONS.

Q. What is the literal meaning of conjunction?

A. It is derived from the Latin *conjungo*, and signifies to join together.

Q. What do conjunctions join?

A. They join together words and sentences; as, James *and* John; Henry writes *and* Thomas reads.

Q. Which are the conjunctions?

A. *And*, which unites the James with John; it is also the conjunction in the second example.

## INTERJECTION.

Q, What am I to understand by an interjection?

A. The word interjection signifies a sudden emotion of the mind connected with grief or joy; as, "*Alas!* For the times so corrupted."

Have you done speaking of the parts of speech?

A. Yes; I have.

Q. Will you, then, before quitting the subject, just give a very brief account of each.

A. Yes.

Q. What have you to say about an article?

A. I have to tell you the articles, only two in number, are always placed before *nouns*, and limit the extension of the nouns in respect of numbers.

Q. What about a noun?

A. That a noun is that which has an independent existence, and admits of being qualified by an *adjective* only.

Q, What of an adjective?

A. That an adjective may be placed either before a *noun* or after it; and it always tells us what sort of a noun it is, whether good or bad.

Q. What about a pronoun?

A. That a personal pronoun is only used for a *noun*.

Q. What about a verb?

A. That a verb signifies *acting* or *doing* in some way or other.

Q. What of an adverb?

A. That an adverb gives some additional circumstance to the three parts of speech to which it is allowed to be joined.

Q. What of a preposition?

A. That a preposition is placed before nouns and pronouns, and points out a relationship.

Q. What of a conjunction?

A. That a conjunction joins together the rest of the parts of speech.

Q. What about an interjection?

A. That an interjection only marks a very peculiar feeling of the mind.

## SYNTAX.

Q. What will you now proceed to consider?

A. Syntax.

Q. What is the meaning of Syntax?

A. Syntax comes from the Greek, and signifies to put in order, to arrange.

Q. What do you mean by Syntax here?

A. Syntax teaches us how to put words in their proper places, by furnishing us with rules.

Q. Will you point out these rules?

A. Yes; I will lay them before you in as few words as I can.

## RULES FOR THE PROPER ARRANGEMENT OF WORDS.

### RULE I.

Every verb must be of the same number and person as its nominative case: as, "Masters command;" "John loves."

### RULE II.

Prepositions and active verbs must be followed by an objective case: as, "I advise you;" "I speak to him." Here the words *you* and *him* are both in the objective case; one being governed by an *active* verb, the other by a preposition.

### RULE III.

Two nouns, coupled by a conjunction, must have nouns, verbs, and pronouns referring to them in the plural number; as, " James *and* John may have a holiday, because they are good boys."

Q. Will you give me a little explanation about this rule?

A. Yes; James and John are the two nouns, coupled by *and :* and as the verb *are* and *they* and boys refer to the two nouns, they are in the plural number.

### RULE IV.

Conjunctions couple the same cases of nouns and tenses of verbs; as, " You *and* I are in good health;" " Love good works *and* hate bad ones."

Q. Does this rule admit of exceptions?

A. Yes; but our space is too short to mention them.

### RULE V.

The verb *to be* is preceded and followed by

D

the same case; as, "It is *I*," and not "It is *me*," because *it* is in the nominative case.

### RULE VI.

Should the present participle be used substantively, it must be preceded by *The* and followed by *Of*, as, it is *the doing of* it.

### RULE VII.

A noun and its pronoun should not be the nominative to the same verb: as, "John, he is good;" it should be, "John is good."

### RULE VIII.

An adjective in the comparative degree and the word *other* should be followed by *than*, and not by *but*, as is often done: as, "He is better than I;" "We have no other book than this."

### RULE IX.

*Such* is followed by *as*, and also by *that:* as, "She is such as I expected; "His treatment was such that I left him."

### RULE X.

Double negatives and double comparatives must not be used : as, "I do not want *no* bread;" "This apple is *more* sweeter." It ought to be, "I do not want any bread;" "This apple is sweeter."

### RULE XI.

Two nouns agree in case when one is explanatory of the other; as, "James, King of England."

### RULE XII.

If the one is not explanatory of the other, the first must be put in the possessive case; as, "John's hat."

### RULE XIII.

The past participle should always be used after the verbs *have* and *be* : as, "I have run," and not "I have ran;" "It must be drunk," and not "It must be drank."

### RULE XIV.

A pronoun must be of the same number, person, and gender as the noun it represents; as, "John came, and *he* is well."

### RULE XV.

The relative must be of the same number, gender, and person as the antecedent; as, "The man *who*."

### RULE XVI.

When a verb is preceded by a singular and a plural nominative, which are separated by *or* or *nor*, the verb must agree with the latter; as, "Neither my *son* nor my *daughters wrote* to me."

### RULE XVII.

Sometimes a sentence, or part of a sentence, is the nominative to a verb; as, "To speak the truth, *is* highly proper."

### RULE XVIII.

The distributive pronouns *each, every, either,* and *neither* agree with nouns and verbs in the singular only; as, "Every man is mortal."

### RULE XIX.

We use *To* after verbs signifying motion; as, "I am going *to* town."

*At*, after the verb *to be;* as, I was at home. *In* is put before the names of countries and large cities: as, *In* America; *In* London. *At* is put before villages, towns, and foreign cities; as, "We were *at* Walton, *at* Liverpool, *at* Rome."

Every sentence implying *future time* and *doubt* ought to be in the subjunctive mood; as, "If he be at home bring him with you."

# APPENDIX.

—o—

Q. What is a *regular* verb?

A. A regular verb is one which makes its past tense and past participle by adding *d,* or *ed,* to the present: as, present, *advise;* past, *advised;* past participle, *advised.*

Q. What is an *irregular* verb?

A. An irregular verb is one which does not make its past tense and past participle by adding *d,* or *ed,* to the present: as, present, *arise;* past, *arose;* past participle, *arisen.*

### LIST OF IRREGULAR VERBS.

| *Present.* | *Past.* | *Past Participle.* |
|---|---|---|
| Abide | abode | abode |
| Am | was | been |
| Arise | arose | arisen |
| Awake | awoke | awaked |
| Beár, *to bring forth* | bore, bare | bôrn |
| Beár, *to carry* | bore, bare | bórne |

| Present. | Past. | Past Participle. |
|---|---|---|
| Beat | beat | beaten, or beat |
| Begin | began | begun |
| Bend | bent | bent |
| Bereave | bereft | bereft |
| Beseech | besought | besought |
| Bid | bad, bade | bidden |
| Bind | bound | bound |
| Bite | bit | bitten, bit |
| Bleed | bled | bled |
| Blow | blew | blown |
| Break | broke | broken |
| Breed | bred | bred |
| Bring | brought | brought |
| Build | built | built |
| Burst | burst | burst |
| Buy | bought | bought |
| Cast | cast | cast |
| Catch | caught | caught |
| Chide | chid | chidden, or chid |
| Choose | chose | chosen |
| Cleave, *to adhere* | clave | cleaved |
| Cleave, *to split* | clove, cleft | cloven, or cleft |
| Cling | clung | clung |
| Clothe | clothed | clad |
| Come | came | come |
| Cost | cost | cost |

| *Present.* | *Past.* | *Past Participle.* |
|---|---|---|
| Crow | crew | crowed |
| Creep | crept | crept |
| Cut | cut | cut |
| Dare, *to venture* | durst | dared |
| Dare, *to challenge* | dared | dared |
| Deal | dealt | dealt |
| Dig | dug, or digged | dug, or digged |
| Do | did | done |
| Draw | drew | drawn |
| Drink | drank | drunk |
| Drive | drove | driven |
| Eat | āte | eaten |
| Fall | fell | fallen |
| Feed | fed | fed |
| Feel | felt | felt |
| Fight | fought | fought |
| Find | found | found |
| Flee | fled | fled |
| Fling | flung | flung |
| Fly | flew | flown |
| Forbear | forbore | forbórne |
| Forget | forgot | forgotten, forgot |
| Forsake | forsook | forsaken |
| Freeze | froze | frozen |
| Get | got | got, gotten |
| Gild | gilt | gilt |

| Present. | Past. | Past Participle. |
|---|---|---|
| Gird | girt | girt |
| Give | gave | given |
| Go | went | gone |
| Grave | graved | graven |
| Grind | ground | ground |
| Grow | grew | grown |
| Hang | hung | hung |
| Have | had | had |
| Hear | heard | heard |
| Hew | hewed | hewn |
| Hide | hid | hidden, or hid |
| Hold | held | held |
| Hurt | hurt | hurt |
| Keep | kept | kept |
| Knit | knit | knit, or knitted |
| Know | knew | known |
| Lade | laded | laden |
| Lay | laid | laid |
| Lead | led | led |
| Leave | left | left |
| Lend | lent | lent |
| Let | let | let |
| Lie, *to lie down* | lay | lain, or lien |
| Load | loaded | laden |
| Lose | lost | lost |
| Make | made | made |

| Present. | Past. | Past Participle. |
| --- | --- | --- |
| Mean | meant | meant |
| Meet | met | met |
| Mow | mowed | mown |
| Pay | paid | paid |
| Put | put | put |
| Quit | quit, or quitted | quit |
| Read | read | read |
| Rend | rent | rent |
| Rid | rid | rid |
| Ride | rode | ridden, or rode |
| Ring | rang, or rung | rung |
| Rise | rose | risen |
| Rive | rived | riven |
| Run | ran | run |
| Saw | sawed | sawn |
| Say | said | said |
| See | saw | seen |
| Seek | sought | sought |
| Seethe | seethed, or sod | sodden |
| Sell | sold | sold |
| Send | sent | sent |
| Set | set | set |
| Shake | shook | shaken |
| Shape | shaped | shapen |
| Shave | shaved | shaven |
| Shear | shore | shŏrn |

| Past. | Past Participle. |
|-------|------------------|
| shed | shed |
| shone | shone |
| shod | shod |
| shot | shot |
| showed | shown |
| shrank, or shrunk | shrunk |
| shred | shred |
| shut | shut |
| sang, or sung | sung |
| sank, or sunk | sunk |
| sat | sitten, or sat |
| slew | slain |
| slept | slept |
| slid | slidden |
| slang, or slung | slung |
| slank, or slunk | slunk |
| slit, or slitted | slit, or slitted |
| smote | smitten |
| sowed | sown |
| spoke, spake | spoken |
| sped | sped |
| spent | speut |
| spilt | spilt |
| span, or spun | spun |
| spat, or spit | spitten, or spit |
| split | split |

| Present. | Past. | Past Participle. |
|---|---|---|
| Spread | spread | spread |
| Spring | sprang, or sprung | sprung |
| Stand | stood | stood |
| Steal | stole | stolen |
| Stick | stuck | stuck |
| Sting | stung | stung |
| Stink | stank, or stunk | stunk |
| Stride | strode, or strid | stridden |
| Strike | struck | struck, stricken |
| String | strang, or strung | strung |
| Strive | strove | striven |
| Strew | strewed | strewed, or strown |
| Strow | strowed | strowed |
| Swear | swore, or sware | sworn |
| Swĕat | sweat | sweat |
| Sweep | swept | swept |
| Swell | swelled | swollen |
| Swim | swam, or swum | swum |
| Swing | swang, or swung | swung |
| Take | took | taken |
| Teach | taught | taught |
| Teār | tore | torn |
| Tell | told | told |
| Think | thought | thought |
| Thrive | throve | thriven |
| Throw | threw | thrown |

| Present. | Past. | Past Participle. |
|---|---|---|
| Thrust | thrust | thrust |
| Tread | trod | trodden |
| Wax | waxed | waxen |
| Weār | wore | wŏrn |
| Weave | wove | woven |
| Weep | wept | wept |
| Win | won | won |
| Wĭnd | wŏûnd | wŏûnd |
| Work | wrought | wrought, worked |
| Wring | wrung | wrung |
| Write | wrote | written |

## DEFECTIVE VERBS.

| Present. | Past. | Past Participle. |
|---|---|---|
| Can | could | ———— |
| May | might | ———— |
| Must | must | ———— |
| Ought | ought | ———— |
| ———— | quoth | ———— |
| Shall | should | ———— |
| Wis | wist | ———— |
| Wit, or wot | wot | ———— |

## RULE I.

Verbs ending in ss, sh, ch, x, or o, form

the third person singular of the Present Indicative, by adding es — thus, He dress-*es*, march-*es*, brush-*es*, go-*es*.

### RULE II.

Verbs in y change y into i before the terminations est, es, eth, and ed; but not before ing;—y, with a vowel before it, is not changed into i—thus

| Present. | Past. | Part. |
|---|---|---|
| Pray, prayest, prays, or prayed. | Prayed. | Praying |
| Try, triest, tries, or trieth. | Tried. | Trying. |

### RULE III.

Verbs accented on the last syllable, and verbs of one syllable, ending in a single consonant, preceded by a single vowel, double the final consonant before the terminations est, eth, ed, ing ; but never before s—thus, allot, allottest, allotteth, allots, allotted, allotting ; blot, blottest, blotteth, blots, blotted, blotting.

### A LIST OF ADVERBS.

Again, ago, almost, alone, already, apart, always, asunder.

Backward, downward, doubtless, daily, ever, enough, exceedingly, first.

Forth, forward, haply, here, hither, how, ill, little.

Less, least, much, more, most, nay, not, no.

Never, now, once, perhaps, peradventure, quite, rather, soon.

Seldom, so, since, still, sometimes, too, then, thus.

Thence, twice, thrice, thither, there, upwards, while, whilst.

Why, well, where, when, whence, whither, yea, yes.

### A LIST OF PREPOSITIONS.

About, above, according to, across, after, against, along, amid, amidst.

Among, amongst, around, at, athwart, bating, before, behind, below.

Beneath, beside, besides, between, betwixt, beyond, by, concerning, down.

During, except, excepting, for, from, in, into instead of, near.

Nigh, of, off, on, over, out of, past, regarding, respecting.

Round, since, through, throughout, till, to, touching, towards, under.

Under, unto, up, upon, with, within, without.

### A LIST OF INTERJECTIONS.

Adieu! ah! alas! alack! away! aha! begone! hark!

Ho! ha! he! hail! halloo! hum! hush! huzza!

Hist! hey-day! lo! O! O, strange! O, brave! pshaw! see! well-a-day!

---

Certain words and phrases which must be followed by appopriate prepositions :—

| | |
|---|---|
| Abhorrence of | Admonish of |
| Abound in, with | Admission to |
| Abridge of, from | Affinity to |
| Assent from | Alienate from |
| Accede to | Alteration in |
| Accord with | Antipathy to |
| Accuse of | Approve of |
| Acquit of | Ask of, for, or after |

Acquiesce in

Adapt to

Adequate to

Adhere to

Averse to

Believe in, on

Betray to

Boast of

Border upon, on

Catch at, with, by

Composed of

Compatible with

Confide in

Congenial to

Consequent upon

Conversant with, in

Correspond with

Depend upon, on

Derogate from

Devolve upon, on

Different from

Diminution of

Discouragement to

Dissent from

Endear to

Engaged in, for

Fall under, from, upon

Aspire to, after

Assent to

Assure of

Attend to

Avert from

Bereft of

Bestow upon, on

Bind to, in

Call upon, on, at, for

Change for

Compliance with

Confer upon, on

Conformable to

Congratulate on, upon

Consonant to

Convince, convict of

Deficient in

Deprive of

Derogatory to

Die of, by, for

Difficulty in

Disappointment in, of

Dispose of

Eager in, for

Endowed with

Expert at, in

Fawn at, on

Greedy after, of

Independent of

Need of

Prejudicial to

Proud of

Pursuant to

Regard to

Significant of

Sympathise with

True to

United with

Want of

Worthy of

Glad at, of

Inculcate upon, on

Made of

Prejudice against

Provide with, for

Pursuance of

Reconcile to

Resolve on

Smile upon, on, at

Triumph over

Trust in, to

Value upon

Wait upon, for, at

Warn of

# MISCELLANEOUS OBSERVATIONS.

Several nouns coming together in the possessive case, an apostrophe with *s* should be annexed only to the last; as, James and John's house. Should words come between the possessive cases, each must have the apostrophe and *s*; as, He gained Jane's, as well as Lucy's, affections.

S is omitted after the apostrophe when the first noun has an *s* in the two last syllables and the following noun begins with *s* ; as, righteousness' sake.

When the following noun does not begin with *s*, the first noun must have *s*, as well as the apostrophe, annexed; as, Norris's invitation.

| | | | |
|---|---|---|---|
| Neither, should be followed by | | | Nor |
| Whether | „ | „ | Or |
| Either | „ | „ | Or |
| Though | „ | „ | Yet |

E

Nouns and numerical adjectives must agree ; as, six feet, and not six foot; ten pounds, and not ten pound.

We apply *which* to inferior animals and things void of life ; we apply it also to *persons* in asking questions : as, The look *which* I had ; the dog *which* you gave me ; *which* of these men is guilty ?

*That* is used in the place of *who,* and *which* after the words *any, same, all, some,* the superlative degree of an adjective, and the interrogative, *who.*

The relative ought to be placed immediately after its antecedent ; as, The man *whom* I saw.

*Superior* and *inferior* should have *to* after them ; as inferior *to* none ; superior *to* all, *Chief, true, perfect, universal,* &c., should not be compared, because, strictly speaking, they do not admit of comparison—that which is true cannot be more than true. Two negatives in English are equal to an affirmative ; as, I *don't want no* water, means, I *want* water.

*Not,* qualifying the present participle is

placed before it; as, *Not being* at home, I was prevented from an interview.

*Never* should not be used for *ever;* as, If I run *never* so fast, it should be *ever* so fast. Avoid using the word *from* before *hence, whence, thence;* as, *Whence* came you? and not, *From* whence came you?

In comparing two objects, use the comparative degree of the adjective, and not the superlative: as, Jane is *younger* than Annie; John is *worse* than George. Should more than two be compared, use the superlative; as, Charles is the *eldest* of the three.

*Who* placed immediately after *than* should be in the nominative, and not in objective case; as, Paul, *than who*, a greater Apostle never lived.

The word that asks and the word which answers to a question must be in the same case; as, *Who* told him? I (told him). *Whose* pen is this? *John's.*

Two persons or things being contrasted, *that* refers to the first-mentioned, *this* to the last; as, There is a great difference between justice and injustice; *that* is right, *this* wrong.

After the past tense of a verb we should use the present, and not the perfect, infinitive : as, I intended to *go* home; and not, I intended to *have gone* home.

The interjections Oh! and ah! require the first personal pronoun to be in the objective case; as, Ah, *me !* Oh, *you* simple ones!

*Ye* may be used as the nominative, but never as the objective case. *You* must be followed by a plural verb, because it is always plural, though applied to a single person. *O !* is used in wishing, exclaiming, or in addressing a person. *Oh!* expresses pain, sorrow, or surprise. *Much* is applied to quantity, *many* to number. Not *less* than fifty, should be, Not *fewer* than fifty. The word *nice* should be applied to what we eat and drink, and not to individuals : as, Tea is *nice ;* and, instead of saying Mr. Willows is a nice man, we should say, Mr. Willows is an *agreeable* man.

We should say, A handsome man, and a beautiful woman; or, if the parties to whom

these epithets are applied, be not justly entitled
to them, we can use another qualifying word,
as the case may require.

| *Improper.* | *Proper.* |
|---|---|
| Two spoonsful | Two spoonfuls |
| I had rather go | I would rather go |
| A new beginner | a beginner |
| The latter end | the end |
| In this here place | in this place |
| Two and three *is* five | two and three *are* five |
| A new pair of boots | a pair of new boots |
| Three last | last three |
| The two first | the first two |
| He pulls flowers | he gathers flowers |
| Who do you speak to ? | to whom do you speak ? |
| If I am not mistaken | if I do not mistake |
| He plunged down into the water | plunged into the water |
| I question the veracity of that affair | I question the truth of that affair (veracity being applied only to persons) |
| It is apparent | it is obvious |
| The subject matter | the subject |
| What may be your name ? | what is your name ? |
| Opposite the palace | opposite to the palace |
| I add one more word | I add one word more |

| *Improper.* | *Proper.* |
|---|---|
| An oldish man | an elderly man |
| Say the grace | say grace |
| Cheese and bread | bread and cheese |
| Milk and bread | bread and milk |
| We will be glad | we shall be glad |
| He is a widow | he is a widower |
| It is equally the same | it is the same |
| Close the door | shut the door |
| A milk cow | a milch cow |
| Give me them pears | give me those pears |
| He ascends up | he ascends |
| He descends down | he descends |
| Between you and I | between you and me |
| I shall come home | I shall return home |
| He writes better than me | he writes better than I |
| The beef is rather saltish | the beef is saltish. Ish and rather have the same signification |
| A child of four years old | a child four years old |
| The above discourse | the preceding discourse |
| All over the country | over all the country |
| I propose going to town | I purpose going to town |
| John and James slew one another | John and James slew each other |
| A large enough number | a number large enough |
| A house to let | a house to be let |

| *Improper.* | *Proper.* |
|---|---|
| I don't like it as well | I don't like it so well |
| As far as I can judge | so far as I can judge |
| In its primary sense | in its primitive sense |
| The house is building | the house is being built |
| Bills are requested to be paid | it is requested that bills be paid |
| He wrote me | he wrote to me |

In speaking, say, The Miss Campbells; in writing, The Misses Campbell.

*Elder* and *eldest* should be applied to persons, *older* and *oldest* to things.

Pronunce the words *one* and *once* as if written *wun* and *wunce: love* as if written *luv; groat* as if written *grawt.*

Every word in the English language beginning with *h* must have the *h* sounded, except the following :—Herb, herbage, heir, heiress, honest, honesty, honor, honorable, honorably, hospital, hostler, hour, hourly, humor, humorist, humorous, humorously, humorsome.

## OF CAPITALS.

The pronoun *I* and the interjection *O!* must be written in capitals.

Common nouns, when personified; as, Come, gentle *Spring*.

The first word of every book, or any other piece of writing, must begin with a capital letter.

Proper names; that is, names of places, persons, ships, &c.

The first word after a period, and the answer to a question, must have capitals.

The first word of every line in poetry.

The appellations of the Deity; as, God, Omnipotent.

Adjectives derived from the proper names of places; as, Grecian, Roman, English, &c.

The first word of a quotation, introduced after a colon; as, Always remember this ancient maxim: " Know thyself."

# PUNCTUATION.

Punctuation teaches us where to insert Points in written composition, in order to make the meaning and construction clear.

> A Comma is marked thus ( , )
> A Semicolon         „        ( ; )
> A Colon             „        ( : )
> A Period or Full Stop        ( . )

## THE USE OF THE COMMA.

A sentence which has but one subject, or nominative, or one finite verb, is called a simple sentence, and does not admit of a pause; as, *Mary loves truth.*

Here, *Mary* is the subject, or nominative case, to the verb *loves*, and *truth* the answer or objective case, after the verb *loves*.

In every sentence there may be as many

distinctions or stops as there are nominative cases or finite verbs expressed or understood; as, *My master, brothers, sisters, children, all respect thee.* The same rule holds good when either the nominative is qualified by several adjectives, or when the verb is modified by adverbs; as, *A good, wise, virtuous man is respected. He studies diligently, constantly, and methodically.*

The first of these sentences is equal to—*My mother respects thee, my sisters respect thee, my children respect thee.* The second to—*A good man is respected, a wise man is respected,* &c. The third to—*He studies diligently, he studies constantly,* &c.

If, however, a conjunction comes between the subjects or qualifying words, the comma is omitted; as, *A wise and good man.* Words in opposition must be separated by a comma; as *John, King of England, is no more.* Also, words in the vocative case: as, *Sir, I hope you are well; James, allow me to accompany you.*

## OF THE SEMICOLON, COLON, AND PERIOD.

A Semicolon is used instead of a comma when the members of the sentence are not so closely connected with each other : as, *The charge of poisoning now only remains to be discussed; of which I can see no foundation.*

When any member of a sentence makes complete sense, and is followed by another member which arises from it, but which is not connected with it in construction, a Colon should be used, as, *The Augustan age was so eminent for good poets, that they have served as models to all others : yet it did not produce any good tragic poets.*

A sentence being complete in sense and construction, must be marked with a Period; as, *Eternity is endless duration.*

All abbreviations have a period after them; as, B.B.

*Exclamation* ( ! ) is used to mark an emotion of the mind.

*Interrogation* ( ? ) is placed after a question.

*Hyphen* ( - ) is used to connect corresponding words ; as, *Doomsday-Book.* It is also used at the end of a line to connect one part of a word to another part beginning the next line.

*Parenthesis* ( ) is used to enclose a remark or sentence in a sentence.

*Apostrophe* ( ' ) is used when a letter is omitted ; as, Belov'd.

*Caret* ( ∆ ) shows a word is omitted or inter-lined.

*Section* ( § ) serves to mark the division of a chapter.

*Paragraph* ( ¶ ) denotes the beginning of a new subject.

*Quotation* ( " " ) is used when the words of another are quoted.

*Index* or *hand* ( ☞ ) points to something of importance.

*Asterisk* ( * )—*Obelisk* ( † )—*Double Dagger* ( ‡ )—and *Parallels* ( ‖ ) refer to some note on the *margin*, or at the bottom of the page.

# AN EXPLANATION

OF

# LATIN PHRASES AND QUOTATIONS.

———o———

*Ab initio,* from the beginning.
*Absit invidia,* all envy apart.
*Ab urbe condita,* from the building of the city.
*Ac etiam,* and also.
*A cruce salus,* salvation from the cross.
*Ad absurdum,* showing the absurdity of a contrary opinion.
*Ad captandum vulgus,* to catch the vulgar.
*Ad infinitum,* to infinity.
*Ad libitum,* at pleasure.
*Ad quod damnum,* to what damage.
*Ad referendum,* to be further considered.
*Ad valorem,* according to the value.
*A fortiori,* with stronger reason.
*Alias,* otherwise.
*Alma mater,* a benign mother; a university.
*Alternis horis,* every other hour.
*A mensa et thoro,* from bed and board.
*Amicus humani generis,* a friend of the human race.
*Amicus curiæ,* a friend of the court.
*Amor patriæ,* the love of our country.
*Anglicé,* in English.
*Anguis latet in herba,* a snake lurks in the grass.
*Animo furandi,* with the intention of stealing.
*Anno domini,* in the year of our Lord.
*A.M., ante meridian,* before noon.
*A posteriori,* from the latter; from behind.
*A priori,* from the former; from before.
*Aqua fortis,* literally, strong water; nitric acid.
*Arcanum,* a secret.
*Arcana imperii,* state secrets.
*Ardentia verba,* glowing words.
*Argumentum ad hominem,* an argument which has a personal
*Audentes fortuna juvat,* fortune assists the daring.    [application.
*Audi alteram partem,* hear the other party.
*Audita querela,* the complaint being heard.
*Aurea mediocritas,* the golden mean.
*Auri sacra fames,* the accursed thirst of gold.
*Aut Cæsar, aut nullus,* he will be Cæsar or nobody.
*A vinculo matrimonii,* from the chain of marriage.

*Bona fide,* in good faith.
*Brutum fulmen,* a harmless thunderbolt.

*Cacoëthes carpendi,* a rage for collecting.
*Cacoëthes loquendi,* a rage for speaking.
*Cacoëthes scribendi,* an itch for writing.
*Cadit questio,* the question falls, or drops.
*Capias,* a law term—you may take.
*Cede Deo,* yield to God or Providence.
*Certum pete finem,* aim at a sure end.
*Cæteris paribus,* the rest being alike, or other things being equal.
*Commune bonum,* a common good.
*Communia proprie dicere,* to express ordinary things with propriety.
*Communibus annis,* one year with another.
*Compos mentis,* a man of sound and composed mind,
*Concordia discors,* a jarring concord.
*Contra bonos mores,* against good manners.
*Cor unum, via una,* one heart, one way.
*Cras credemus, hodie nihil,* to-morrow we shall believe, but
*Credula res amor est,* love is credulous.       [nothing to-day.
*Cui bono,* to what good will it tend?
*Cui malo,* to what evil?
*Currente calamo,* literally, with a running pen; with great
*Custos rotulorum,* the keepers of the rolls.       [expedition.

*Data,* things granted.
*Data fata secutus,* following his declared fate.
*Deceptio visus,* a visual illusion.
*De facto,* from the fact, in reality.
*De jure,* from the law.
*De mortuis nil nisi bonum,* of the dead let nothing be said but
*Deo juvante,* with God's assistance.       [what is favorable.
*Deo favente,* with God's favor.
*Deo non fortuna,* from God, not fortune.
*Deo volente,* God willing,
*Desunt cætera,* the rest is wanting.
*Dii penates,* household gods.
*Divide et impera,* divide and govern,
*Dominus providebit,* the Lord will provide,
*Ducit amor patriæ,* the love of my country leads me.
*Dulce et decorum est pro patria mori,* it is pleasing and honorable
to die for one's country.
*Dum spiro, spero,* whilst I breathe, I hope.
*Dum vivimus vivamus,* whilst we live, let us live.
*Duos qui sequitur lepores neutrum capit,* he who follows two
hares is sure to catch neither.
*Durante bene placito,* during good pleasure.

*Durante vita,* during life.
*Durum telum necessitas,* necessity is a hard weapon.


*Ecce homo,* behold the man.
*Eo instante,* at that instant.
*Eo nomine,* by that name.
*Esto perpetua,* be thou perpetual.
*Esto quod esse videris,* be what you seem.
*Et cetera,* and the rest.
*Et decus et pretium recti,* the ornament and the reward of virtue.
*Et sic de semilibus,* and so of the like.
*Ex cathedra,* from the chair.
*Ex curea,* out of court.
*Ex cerpta,* extracts from a work.
*Ex concesso,* from what has been granted.
*Exempli gratia, E.G.,* for the sake of example.
*Exemplo plus quam ratione vivimus,* we live more by example
*Ex gratia,* out of favor, from courtesy.          [than precept.
*Ex mero motu,* from a mere notion.
*Ex necessitate rei,* from the necessity of the case.
*Ex nihilo nihil fiat,* nothing can come of nothing.
*Ex officio,* by virtue of office.
*Ex parte,* on one side only.
*Ex tempore,* off hand; without deliberation.


*Fac simile,* an exact copy.
*Fallentis semita vitæ,* the deceitful path of life.
*Fari quæ sentiat,* to speak what he thinks.
*Fata obstant,* the fates oppose it.
*Favete linguis,* literally, from our tongue; be attentive.
*Fax mentis incendium gloriæ,* the torch of the mind is the flame
*Faex populi,* the dregs of the people.          [of glory.
*Felicitas multos habet amicos,* prosperity has many friends.
*Felix qui nihil debit,* happy is the man who owes nothing.
*Felo de se,* self murder.
*Feræ naturæ,* of a wild nature.
*Fiat,* let it be done.
*Fiat justitia, ruat cœlum,* let justice be done, though the heavens
*Fiat lux,* let there be light.          [should fall.
*Fide et fortitudine,* by faith and fortitude.
*Fide et fiducia,* by faith and courage.
*Fideli certa merces,* the faithful are certain of reward.
*Fidelis ad urnum,* faithful to death.
*Fideliter,* faithfully.
*Fide et amore,* by faith and love.
*Fidus et audax,* faithful and intrepid.
*Finem respice,* look to the end.

*Flagrante bello,* literally, while the war is burning; during
*Flecti non frangi,* to bend, not to break.                    [hostilities.
*Fortes fortuna juvat,* fortune favors the bold.
*Forti et fideli nil difficile,* nothing is difficult to the brave and
*Fortiter et recte,* courageously and honestly.                [faithful.
*Fortiter geret crucem,* he will bravely support the cross.
*Fortitudine et prudentia,* by fortitude and prudence.
*Fortuna sequatur,* let fortune follow.
*Fortunæ cœtera mando,* I commit the rest to fortune.
*Fortunæ filius,* a son of fortune.
*Fuit Ilium,* literally, Troy was; used figuratively to express that
something is now no more.
*Furor loquendi,* an eagerness for speaking.
*Furor scribendi,* an itch for writing.


*Gaudet tentamine virtus,* virtue rejoices in temptation.
*Gratis,* for nothing.
*Gratis dictum,* said for nothing.
*Gravis ira regum semper,* the anger of kings is always severe.


*Haud passibus æquis,* not with equal steps.
*Hic et ubique,* here and there and everywhere.
*Hic finis fandi,* here there was an end of the discourse.
*Hoc age,* do or mind this.
*Hodie mihi, cras tibi,* to-day it belongs to me, to-morrow to you.
*Homo multarum literarum,* a learned man.
*Humanum est errare,* it is the lot of humanity to err.


*Ibid, Ibidem,* in the same place.
*I.e., id est,* that is.
*Ignis fatuus,* wild fire ; Will o' the Wisp.
*Ignoramus,* an uninformed blockhead.
*Impromptu,* on the spur of the moment.
*In cœlo quies,* there is rest in heaven.
*In hoc signo spes mea,* in this sign is my hope.
*In te, Domine, speravi,* in thee, O Lord, have I put my trust.
*Inter nos,* between ourselves.
*In utroque fidelis,* faithful to both.
*Ipso facto,* by the fact itself.
*Ipso jure,* by the law itself.
*Ira brevis furor,* anger is short madness.
*Ita lex scripta est,* thus says the law.


*Jacta est alea,* the die is cast.
*Judex damnatur cum nocens absolvitur,* the judge is found guilty
when the criminal is acquitted.
*Judicium parium,* the judgment of our peers.

*Jure humano,* by human law.
*Jure divino,* by divine law.
*Jus civile,* the civil law.
*Jus gentium,* the law of nations.
*Jus sanguinis,* the right of blood.
*Justitiæ soror fides,* faith is the sister of justice.

*Labor omnia vincit,* labor overcomes everything.
*Lapsus linguæ,* a slip of the tongue.
*Laus Deo,* praise to God.
*Lex talionis,* the law of retaliation.
*Libertus et natale solum,* liberty and my native soil.
*Litera scripta manet,* a written letter remains.
*Locum tenens,* literally, holding the place ; a deputy or substitute.
*Ludere cum sacris,* literally, to sport with holy things; to jest
*Magna Charta,* the great charter.                        [profanely.
*Malum in se,* a thing evil in itself.
*Manu forte,* with a brave hand.
*Mens sana in corpore sano,* a sound mind in a sound body.
*Multum in parvo,* much in little.

*Necessitas non habet legem,* necessity has no law.
*Ne plus ultra,* nothing more beyond.
*Ne quid nimis,* too much of one thing is good for nothing.
*Non sibi, sed patriæ,* not for himself, but for his country.
*Nosce teipsum,* know thyself.
*Nota bene (N.B.)* mark well.

*Odi profanum vulgus,* I hate the profane vulgar.
*Omnia vincit amor,* love conquers all things.
*Opera pretium est,* literally, it is the price of labor; it is worth
one's while.
*Peccavi,* I have sinned.
*Per fas et nefas,* through right and wrong.
*Permitte cætera divis,* leave the rest to the gods.
*Per se,* by itself.
*P.M., Post Meridian,* afternoon.
*Prima facie,* on the first view.
*Principiis obsta,* oppose mischief in the beginning.
*Pro bono publico,* for the public good.
*Pro et con,* for and against.
*Pro tempore,* for the time.

*Quantum,* due proportion.
*Quid nunc,* what now; applied to a person who is much
*Quid pro quo,* what for what; tit for tat.       [occupied in news.
*Quo animo,* with what intention.

*Quo jure,* by what right.
*Quot homines, tot sententiæ,* so many men, so many opinions.

*Rara fides,* good faith.
*Res adversæ,* adversity.
*Res angustæ domi,* poverty.
*Res secundæ,* prosperity.
*Requiescat in pace,* may he rest in peace.
*Respice finem,* look to the end.
*Res publica,* the commonwealth.

*Semper idem,* always the same.
*Servabo fidem,* I will keep my faith.
*Sic passim,* so everywhere.
*Simplex munditiis,* simple in neatness.
*Sine qua non,* literally, without which it cannot be; an indis-
*Spes mea in Deo,* my hope is in God.          [pensable condition.
*Spero meliora,* I hope for better things.
*Statu quo,* in the state in which they formerly were.
*Sua cuique voluptas,* literally, his own pleasure to every one;
every one has a taste for a particular pleasure.
*Suaviter in modo, fortiter in re,* gentle in manner, but vigorous
*Summum bonum,* the chief good.          [in action.

*Tempora mutanta,* the times are changed.
*Tempus edax rerum,* time is the devourer of all things.
*Toga virilis,* the manly robe.

*Uberrima fides,* full faith.
*Ult., ultimus,* the last.

*Vade mecum,* go with me; a constant companion.
*Veni, vidi, vici,* I came, I saw, I conquered.
*Veritas vincit,* truth conquers.
*Vice versa,* the reverse.
*Vide,* see.
*Viz., videlicet,* to wit.
*Vis inertiæ,* the force of indolence.
*Vitæ summa brevis,* the span of life is short.
*Viva voce,* by the living voice, orally.
*Vox populi, vox Dei,* the voice of the people is the law of God.